Swing Otto Swing!

Swing Otto Swing!

story and pictures by
DAVID MILGRIM

Atheneum Books for Young Readers

New York London Toronto Sydney

Atheneum Books for Young Readers
An imprint of Simon & Schuster Children's Publishing Division
1230 Avenue of the Americas
New York, New York 10020

Book design by Sonia Chaghatzbanian
The text for this book is set in Century Old Style.
The illustrations are rendered in digital pen-and-ink.
Printed in the United States of America
First Edition

1 2 3 4 5 6 7 8 9 10

Library of Congress Cataloging-in-Publication Data
Milgrim, David.
Swing Otto swing / David Milgrim.—1st ed.
p.   cm.
Summary: When Otto has trouble learning
to swing on vines like his monkey friends,
he decides to make his own swing set instead.
ISBN 0-689-85564-8
[1. Monkeys—Fiction. 2. Swings—Fiction.] I. Title.
PZ7 .M59485Sw 2004
[E]—dc21   2003001117

FOR
ELLIOT

See Flip.

See Flip swing.

See Flop.

See Flop swing.

See Otto.

See Otto swing.

Hello, Otto.

Good-bye, Otto.

See Flip
give Otto
some tips.

See Otto try again.

See Flip and Flop
give Otto more tips.

See Otto learn.
Learn, Otto, learn.

See Otto swing . . .

See Otto saw.
Saw, saw, saw.

See Otto tie.
Tie, tie, tie.

See Otto swing.
Swing, Otto, swing!